TIME SPIES
Secret in the Tower

By Candice Ransom
Illustrated by Greg Call

MIRRORSTONE

SECRET IN THE TOWER

©2006 Wizards of the Coast, Inc.

Cover and Interior art by Greg Call
First Printing: September 2006
Library of Congress Catalog Card Number: 2005935557

9 8 7 6 5 4 3 2 1

ISBN-10: 0-7869-4027-1
ISBN-13: 978-0-7869-4027-1
620-95555740-001-EN

U.S., CANADA,
ASIA, PACIFIC, & LATIN AMERICA
Wizards of the Coast, Inc.
P.O. Box 707
Renton, WA 98057-0707
+1-800-324-6496

EUROPEAN HEADQUARTERS
Hasbro UK Ltd
Caswell Way
Newport, Gwent NP9 0YH
Great Britain
Please keep this address for your records

Visit our website at **www.mirrorstonebooks.com**

To Kathi:

teacher, fellow writer, good friend

Contents

The End of the World

Alex Chapman felt like he was entering a strange, new land.

He had never seen so many trees and fields. So few houses. No stores. Only a gas station once in a while.

"Cows." His sister Mattie sat up and looked out the car window. "Nothing but cows."

"There's a horse," Alex said.

"You know what I mean." She flashed

him her stern, I'm-a-year-older-than-you look. "I can't believe they're doing this to us. It's the end of the world."

"Maybe not," said Alex. In his stomach, he felt excitement mingle with nervousness. Kind of like the way he felt on Halloween. "It might be an adventure."

"Adventure? Oh, what do you know? You're only eight." She slumped back against the seat.

"Are you guys awake?" their dad asked, glancing at them in his rearview mirror. "Need a rest stop?"

"Where?" asked Mattie. "I don't see a McDonald's."

"Old MacDonald's, maybe." Alex laughed. "Get it? Cows? Old MacDonald's farm?"

"How can you make jokes?" Mattie asked. "We'll never see our friends again. We'll never play soccer again. We'll have to go to . . . a one-room schoolhouse!"

Mr. Chapman laughed. "Mattie, we're moving to Virginia, not the Wild West."

A few months ago, Mr. and Mrs. Chapman had done something unthinkable. They had both quit their jobs and bought a giant, old house in Virginia. Alex had felt like it was the end of the world last month, as he watched the moving van drive away with his computer, his bed, and all his books and toys.

He remembered waving to his mom and dad and his younger sister Sophie, as they pulled out of the driveway to follow the van. He and his older sister Mattie were staying behind in Maryland with their neighbors, the Tuthills, so they could finish up the last month of school.

While Mr. and Mrs. Chapman were busy painting and putting up wallpaper, preparing the house for its new life as an inn, the Tuthills took Alex and Mattie to school, soccer practice, and the movies. They had stayed with the Tuthills until this morning, when their father had arrived to take them to the new house.

"Trust me, Mattie," Mr. Chapman said now, turning off the main highway onto a narrow paved road. "You're going to love it. There are no neighbors for miles around, and at night it's so quiet you can hear yourself think . . ."

Mattie leaned over to whisper to Alex, "Everything about this house sounds so boring!"

"And wait till you see how we've fixed up the old place," Mr. Chapman finished. "Sophie is crazy about it."

"She's only five," Mattie said, as if that explained Sophie's weird likes and dislikes. "What was wrong with our old house anyway?"

"Remember we talked about this?" Mr. Chapman sighed. "Your mother and I needed a change."

"So why couldn't they just paint the front door or something?" Mattie whispered to Alex.

Alex shrugged. He sort of wanted a change, too, but he would miss playing soccer. He was the best goalie on the team at Frost Elementary.

Mr. Chapman turned off the narrow road onto a long, gravel driveway, and said, "This is it."

Alex noticed the sign right away. A dark gray horse's head was painted above the words *Gray Horse Inn*. Bushes and shrubs grew along the driveway in a tangled mass. Honeysuckle vines reached for the car. The sweet scent was so strong it almost made him dizzy.

Their car rounded a curve and an old house came into view. Alex stared. Even Mattie was speechless.

The three-story stone house stood before a mountain carpeted with green trees. The house's windows were long and skinny, and one was round. A small porch capped with a triangular roof stood in front of a red door. On one side, a tower stretched toward the overcast sky. Ivy crept up the tower.

"We have a mountain in our backyard?" Alex asked. "Is it ours?"

Mr. Chapman shut off the car's engine. "It is, actually. Seventy-two acres came with the house."

Alex looked back at the gray stone house.

This was no ordinary house. It was like—a person, he thought. He could almost feel it breathe, sense its heartbeat. This house had things to say. And he couldn't wait to hear them.

He popped the door handle and jumped out of the car.

The front door of the house opened, and Sophie ran down the porch steps. She dragged her stuffed elephant by one leg. Sophie never went anywhere without Ellsworth.

"Mom says hurry up for breakfast," she said. "And no fighting. A man spended the night, and he's eating with us."

"What man?" asked Mattie.

"Our first guest," Mr. Chapman replied, taking suitcases from the trunk. "He came last night in the storm. It was raining so hard, we couldn't turn him away, even though he didn't have a reservation."

Sophie looked around the yard. "Where's the horse?"

"What horse?" Alex asked.

"The horse," Sophie repeated, as if they should know what she was talking about. "I saw her last night. I want to ride her."

"Soph, the only horse is on the sign," Alex said.

"No, this was a real horse," Sophie insisted.

"You must have been dreaming." Mattie sighed. "Come on. Let's get this over with."

The kids walked into the house. Sophie led them into the dining room.

A large table sat in the center of a room with butter yellow walls. Pink and yellow dishes gleamed on green placemats. A pitcher of pink roses stood on an antique sideboard. The table was set for breakfast—scrambled eggs, crisp bacon, toast, and jam.

A young man sat at one end of the table. He gazed out the window as he sipped coffee. That was ordinary enough.

But what he wore was anything but ordinary.

Mrs. Chapman bustled in from the kitchen with a basket of muffins.

"You're here!" she said, giving Alex and

Mattie a quick kiss. "I missed you so much. Look! We have our very first guest. It was pouring last night when I heard a knock on the door. This young man saw our sign. He insisted on sleeping in the Jefferson Room. It wasn't quite ready, but he didn't mind. Don't you love what we've done to the place?" she finished in a rush.

"We haven't seen much—" Alex began.

"Take the grand tour later," said Mrs. Chapman. "Sit down and eat. You must be starving. And say hello to Mr. Jones. Mr. Jones, this is Mattie and Alex."

"Nice to meet you," said Mr. Jones. "I just met Winchester. I thought he was a cushion."

From a chair in the corner, a cat opened one green eye and stared at him. Then he yawned and went back to sleep.

Alex and Mattie chose seats across from

the weirdly dressed guest. Alex reached for a muffin the same time Mattie did.

Sophie slid into the chair next to Mr. Jones. "Are you in a play?"

"Sort of," said Mr. Jones, buttering a muffin. "I'm a re-enactor. I dress and act like a soldier in the Revolutionary War. The Battle of Yorktown is being re-enacted this weekend, and I'm playing a soldier in it."

"I know about the Revolutionary War," Alex said as he heaped his plate with bacon and eggs. "We learned about it in school. The colonies didn't like the British telling them what to do. So we had a war to get our freedom. And Thomas somebody wrote the Declamation of Independence."

"Thomas *Jefferson* wrote the Declaration of Independence," Mattie said. "Were you asleep in social studies?"

"I was awake, smarty!" Alex said. "It's just that—sometimes history is kind of boring."

"History isn't boring," said Mr. Jones. "It's not just dates and battles and generals— history is full of stories about real people."

"Well, I paid attention in school," Mattie said. "There was this guy named Paul Revere. He made a famous ride to warn people the British were coming."

"Did you know a Virginian warned people about the British too?" said Mr. Jones.

Mattie shook her head. "No. I thought the war happened up north, around Boston and stuff."

Mr. Jones smiled. "Well, fighting took place in the Southern States too. Jack Jouett was a captain in the Virginia militia. One night he heard some British officers talking in a tavern not far from this house. They said they were

12

going to kidnap Thomas Jefferson and other men who were fighting for freedom."

"What happened?" asked Mattie.

"Jack jumped on his horse and rode all night," said Mr. Jones. "He went to Thomas Jefferson's house first to warn him, then dashed off to warn the others."

"Did anybody get kidnapped?" Alex asked hopefully.

Mr. Jones reached over and took a postcard from a stack on the sideboard. He removed a pen inside his blue coat before answering.

"No," he said. "Thanks to Jack Jouett, some of the most important men in our country's history were saved."

Mr. Jones studied the photograph on the postcard.

"That's our house," Alex said. It felt funny

to say that. He hadn't slept one single night here.

Mr. Jones nodded. "This is a very old house. I think it was built around the same time as Thomas Jefferson's house, Monticello. It isn't far from here." Uncapping his felt tip pen, he began scribbling on the blank side of the postcard.

"What are you writing?" asked Sophie.

"A note to a friend," Mr. Jones answered. "He's a fellow re-enactor, but he couldn't come this time. I'm telling him about the Gray Horse Inn. If he ever comes this way, he'll want to stay here too." Mr. Jones capped his pen and put it back in his pocket. "Well, Yorktown is a long drive from here. I'd better get going."

He stuck a stamp on the postcard and dropped it on a silver tray on the sideboard by the door. A sign by the tray said, "For Outgoing

Mail." Then he clumped upstairs.

"He's pretty cool!" Alex said. "I hope all of our guests will be pretend soldiers."

"I hope not," said Mattie. "I'm going up-stairs to unpack."

She rose and walked over to the narrow sideboard, then casually glanced at the post-card in the silver tray.

Her eyes grew round.

The Door
in the Wall

"What?" asked Alex.

Mattie jabbed the postcard with her finger.

Alex went over to the table. He stared at the postcard.

The scene on the back had changed. It was no longer a photograph of the Gray Horse Inn.

Alex turned the postcard over. The message was written in fine, spidery cursive. He couldn't read the signature. But it was the postcard Mr. Jones had written, all right.

"The picture changed!" he whispered in awe. "How?"

"I don't know," Mattie said. "If this is a joke, it's not funny. And if it isn't—well, I want to know who did it."

Sophie pretended to feed a bite of muffin to Ellsworth. "It was Mr. Jones."

"Mr. Jones switched cards?" Alex asked. "Is that what you mean, Sophie? That he put another postcard in the basket?"

"No." Sophie dabbed at Ellsworth's mouth with her napkin.

"He couldn't have switched cards," Mattie said firmly. "I watched him. He put the Gray Horse Inn postcard in the basket. I saw him."

"Did you read the message he wrote?" Alex asked her.

"Of course not!" Mattie said. "What kind of a person do you think I am?"

Alex thrust the postcard under her nose. "Read it now. The writing is too weird."

"It doesn't have a date," Mattie said. Then she read the message aloud.

Dear Father,

We have bombed the town all this day. No sign of Cornwallis. He cannot escape by the river or he will be fired upon by French warships. And if he tries to escape by land, he will meet a formidable foe. I must return to my duty.

Yours in haste, Will

"Mr. Jones told us he was writing to his friend about staying here," Alex said. "But what's all this stuff about warships and bombs? What's a formidable foe?"

"An enemy that can't be beat." Mattie squinted at the message. "Even the handwriting is different. Mr. Jones printed with a felt tip pen, but this writing is fancy. And written in blobby ink."

Alex looked at the picture again. "It sounds like the person who wrote the card is in a battle. But who would write a postcard in the middle of a battle?"

"It doesn't make sense," Mattie agreed. "There's only one thing to do . . . go ask Mr. Jones. He should still be in his room."

"Sophie, which room is Mr. Jones in?" Alex asked.

"I'll show you," Sophie said.

The kids tore out of the dining room. They passed through the living room, where comfy chairs sat around a fireplace with a blue-painted mantel. With Sophie in the lead, they charged up a wide, curving staircase. Sunlight poured through the round window on the landing.

Sophie stopped to gaze down at the tangled garden. "Look! There's my horse!" she said.

Alex glanced out the window. "I don't see any horse."

"Way over there. See it?"

Mattie pulled her little sister away from the window. "We don't have time now. We have to find Mr. Jones."

On the second floor, the hall branched into two smaller passages.

"This place is huge!" Alex said.

Sophie pointed down the first hall. "That way's my room. And Mattie's. And yours."

"Where's Mr. Jones's room?" Mattie asked.

"This way." Sophie led them down the second hall. "The people who spend the night sleep here."

Doors with names painted over them stood open. The Dogwood Room was decorated in shades of pink and white. A vase of artificial dogwood blossoms graced a table.

The Cardinal Room had red drapes and pictures of birds on the walls. The Foxhound Room sported a brass hunting horn over its fireplace.

Now Sophie skipped up a straight, narrow staircase at the end of the hall.

Alex was panting by the time they reached the third floor. This house is too big, he thought. Too many stairs, too many doors.

Only one room occupied the third floor. Painted above its door were the words:

"I *cannot live without books*."
—*Thomas Jefferson*

"This is Mr. Jones's room," said Sophie. "Mom calls it the Jefferson Room."

Alex peered inside. A yellow comforter

had been pulled up over a simple four-poster bed. Books and pewter cups lined the fireplace mantle. An old map of Virginia hung on one wall next to an antique clock.

The only figure in the room was a marble statue of a man's head. It stood on a table in front of a window. A sign beneath it read: "Thomas Jefferson: Governor of Virginia, Third President of the United States."

"Mr. Jones isn't here!" Mattie said.

"He must have gone already," Alex said.

She shook her head. "We heard him go upstairs. But he didn't come back down. We would have seen him."

"There are a zillion doors here," Alex pointed out. "Mr. Jones could have gone through another door and we missed him."

Sophie spoke up. "Maybe Mr. Jones is in the other room."

"What other room?" asked Mattie. "We've seen them all."

Sophie shook her head stubbornly. "We haven't seen the room in the tall part."

"The tall part . . ." Mattie said. "You mean the tower?"

"The tower is on this side of the house," Alex said. "There must be another room up here! The door to it has to be right across the hall."

They hurried out of the yellow room and into the hall. But there was no other door. The wall across from the stairs was blank except for a two-shelf bookcase. One shelf held a small stack of old books.

Alex couldn't believe his eyes. "Who would build a room without a door?"

"Maybe the guy who built the house did it for a joke," Mattie said.

Alex tapped on the wall with his knuckles.

Thunk, thunk, thunk.

"Listen. It's hollow. There's a room on the other side, all right. But how do we get inside?"

"Who cares? If we can't get in, obviously Mr. Jones didn't either," Mattie said. "This is stupid. I'm going down to unpack."

Alex quit rapping. A buzzing sensation rippled through his body. It seemed to come from the floorboards beneath his feet.

"You look weird," Mattie said, staring at him. "Are you sick or something?"

"Shhh." He stood still and listened.

His feet were being directed toward the blank wall. He shuffled closer. The tower room—or something inside it—was calling, urging him to find a way in.

"What is with you?" Mattie said.

"I have the weirdest feeling," he said in a

hushed tone. "I think we're supposed to get inside the tower room."

"Says who?" Mattie asked.

"The . . ." Alex hesitated. "The house."

Mattie looked at him skeptically. "Is this like the time you tried to touch the end of the rainbow? You were such a dork—riding your bike like a maniac for five blocks."

Alex winced. He had tried to touch the end of the rainbow. He'd pedaled his bike furiously through their neighborhood. But it had disappeared by the time he jumped off his bike, by the Tuthills' garage. He'd felt like an idiot.

But even though a talking house sounded stranger than chasing rainbows, he firmly believed they had to find a way into the tower room.

"Come on, Mattie," Alex said. "Anything could be in there. A treasure map, maybe even a chest of jewels hidden by an eccentric millionaire."

Mattie crossed her arms over her chest. "So does the house tell us *how* to get in the room?"

"There must be a door here somewhere." He ran his hands along the surface of the wall. "Like a hidden panel. Old houses are loaded with secret panels and stuff."

Mattie stared at the wall. "I don't see any lines that could be a door. And I don't see any hinges."

"Maybe we have to chant some magic words to make a door appear," Alex said.

Sophie sat down on the hall rug and propped Ellsworth on the bottom shelf of the low bookcase.

"Hi, Winchester," she said.

The big cat had followed them upstairs.

Curious, he began smelling the edge of the bottom shelf. His long white whiskers blew backward, just a bit, as if he were standing in a gentle breeze.

Sophie held her hand up to the crack between the side of the shelf and the wall.

"I feel air," she said.

"That's it!" Alex said. "The door's not in the wall. It's in the bookcase! Soph, you're a genius."

Mattie studied the bookcase. The top shelf reached just above her knees. White-painted boards surrounded the bookcase. She bent down. She put her face close to the crack between the side of the bookcase and the white boards.

"I feel air too," she said. "Alex, do you think you can move the bookcase?"

Kneeling, Alex pushed on the bookcase

with both hands. It did not give an inch. He butted it with his shoulder. The bookcase still did not budge.

"It's not moving!" he said.

"What if it's locked from the inside?" Mattie suggested.

"If somebody locked it from the inside, they'd still be in there," Alex said.

They stared at each other.

"That's where Mr. Jones is," said Mattie. "He's really a ghost. He walked right through the wall, and he's waiting for us—"

"Maybe we don't want to go in the room after all," said Alex with a shudder.

Sophie picked at the edge of the book-case with her small fingers. "I bet it's painted shut, like some of the windows downstairs. Daddy had a hard time unsticking them."

"We'll all push." Mattie got down on her

knees and pulled Sophie down beside her. "Come on, Soph."

Alex leaned his shoulder into the bookcase. Mattie leaned against him, and Sophie leaned against Mattie. Winchester looked at them all as if this were a new game.

"On the count of three," said Alex. "One, two—three!"

Alex gave the bookcase a mighty shove. The books on the shelf went flying. One nearly hit Winchester on the head. The cat took off in a blur of black and white paws.

Alex didn't even notice. Breathless, he gaped at the bookcase.

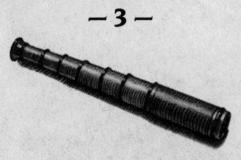

The Secret
in the Tower

The shelves swiveled into a dark opening in the wall.

"It spins open from the middle of the bookcase," Alex said. "Whoever invented this was really smart." On his hands and knees, he headed into the opening. "Come on."

With Ellsworth tucked in the crook of her arm, Sophie crawled in after him, with Mattie not far behind.

Alex stood up. The morning sun had not yet reached this side of the house. But light filtered through the tall windows on the three outside walls of the square tower.

Dust pillowed the windowsills like drifted snow and lay in heaps all over the bare floor. Mattie sneezed three times, but the dust didn't bother Alex.

From outside, Alex heard the faint *rrrr-rrr* as his father started the lawn mower.

The only object in the room was a tall desk with two rows of tiny drawers on top. A wide piece of wood slanted over three bigger drawers at the bottom.

"What a rip-off," Alex said. "Not a speck of treasure."

Mattie sneezed again. "I've never seen so much dust in my life!"

"Maybe the treasure's in here." Sophie reached for the little drawers at the top of the desk. "Look!"

Eagerly, Alex opened the little drawers, one after the other. Ten little drawers in two rows. It seemed to take forever.

Mattie came over and pulled down the slanted piece of wood on the front of the desk. The drop-leaf formed a writing ledge.

Inside the desk were more tiny cubbyholes. She began poking in them.

"Any luck?" Alex asked, closing the last drawer with a sigh.

"Not unless this paperclip is solid gold." Closing the-drop leaf, Mattie checked the bigger drawers below. The first two slid open easily. But they were empty.

She tugged at the bottom drawer, but could not get it open. "This one's jammed."

Alex jiggled and prodded, but the stubborn drawer refused to give. Frustrated, he gave the desk drawer his best soccer kick.

A tiny panel in the side of the desk popped open.

Mattie gasped. "A secret panel!" she exclaimed. "And there's something in here." Reaching inside, she pulled out a narrow wooden box.

The box was made of smooth, satiny wood, with brass corners. Two brass latches shaped like question marks held the lid closed.

"The treasure!" said Alex. His heart thumped. Maybe they had found a diamond necklace worth a fortune!

With trembling fingers, Mattie unhooked the latches and lifted the lid of the box.

Inside, nestled in dark green velvet, was a dull brass tube.

"Some treasure," she said. "What is this thing?"

"It's a spyglass!" said Alex. "Cool!"

Mattie picked up the tube and pulled out the sections, extending it to its full length of about sixteen inches.

"What's a spyglass?" asked Sophie. "Are spies in it?"

"No, it's like a telescope," Mattie explained. "Captains on ships used these to look long distances."

"Let me see it," said Alex.

Mattie handed over the spyglass.

Alex aimed the telescope out the window and peered into the eyepiece. The tube felt strangely warm. His hand tingled.

"Give it back," said Mattie.

He shook his fingers. "Did you feel something odd?"

"Like what?"

"Warm and—kind of alive," he replied.

"Honestly, Alex. You are getting so weird!" She reached for the spyglass.

Alex held it above his head. "I haven't looked through it yet!"

"You did too!" Mattie said.

"I want to see!" Sophie chimed in. "My

turn!" She hopped up and down.

Beneath Alex's fingers, the brass case felt warmer, almost hot. His hand tingled, as if an army of fire ants were crawling over it.

"I'm still looking at it," he said. But Mattie grabbed it away from him. He snatched it back with Sophie hanging on his sleeve.

Whoosh!

Suddenly Alex tumbled downward, as if the floor had opened beneath his feet. He twisted and swooped through a tunnel. Bright colors sparked behind his eyelids. His arms flew out to break his fall.

"Mattie!" he called. "Sophie!" But he was all alone in the tunnel.

4

Riders
in the Night

The twirling stopped. The sparks of color vanished. Alex's feet were planted firmly again.

At first, he couldn't see a thing. Slowly, his eyes adjusted to the dim light. He made out the shape of a lumpy bed. He was in a room, but not the tower room.

Someone sneezed. Mattie.

"Sophie?" Alex whispered. A small hand

curled into his. Sophie was right beside him, clinging to Ellsworth.

He faced a rectangle of light, a doorway. "Do you think we found a secret room underneath the tower room?" Alex asked.

"I don't know." Mattie wrinkled her nose. "This room smells funny. Old. A lot older than the tower room. I wonder what's out there." She pointed at the door.

Alex collapsed the spyglass and put it in his pocket. Then he took a few steps toward the door and stuck his head out. Crude stairs led down a single flight.

"Follow me," he whispered. "But don't talk until we find out where we are."

The kids crept down the stairs. Halfway down, Alex signaled them to stop.

The partial wall of the stairwell shadowed them.

By stooping a little, they could see into two rooms. The first contained a bed, table, and chairs. The furniture looked crude and homemade.

In the second room, a pot hung over a crackling fire in the fireplace. A woman bent over the pot, stirring. She wore a long brown dress, a white apron, and a white ruffled cap. On the table behind her, a candle sputtered.

Alex stared at the fireplace. It looked familiar. Wooden brackets were mounted over the blue-painted mantel.

Somewhere out of sight a door slammed. A boy clumped into the kitchen carrying a lantern. He wore knee pants, white stockings, and buckled shoes. His black hair was tied back in a ponytail. His clothes reminded Alex of Mr. Jones.

"Did you milk the cows already, Michael?" the woman asked, not turning around.

"Mother!" the boy said, putting the lantern on the table. "Father and I just heard that the British are on the road to Charlottesville! They are that close!"

The woman whirled from the pot with a frightened look. "It's not true!"

The door slammed again. This time a man clopped into the kitchen. He took off his hat.

Then he placed his gun in the brackets over the fireplace.

"Michael says the British are coming," the woman said to the man. "What will happen to us?"

"Don't worry," he told her. "I believe they chase more important quarry."

Alex poked Mattie. "What's 'quarry?'" he whispered.

"It's something you hunt," she whispered back.

The woman spooned mush into bowls and set them on the table. The man and boy pulled up a bench and sat down to eat.

"Farmer Miller was at the Cuckoo last night," said the man. "He claimed he saw a large group of British soldiers on horseback."

"Can you trust tavern talk?" the woman asked.

The man nodded. "We can trust Miller. He saw Tarleton and his men, all right."

"Colonel Tarleton is the worst of the worst," Michael, the boy, added.

Alex leaned forward to see him better. The stairs creaked.

Michael jerked his head toward the stairs. Alex ducked into the shadows. Mattie pulled Sophie back.

When the family began talking again, Mattie whispered in Alex's ear. "Do you know where we are?"

"Somebody's house," he said.

"That much I can figure out. But whose house? Who are those people? And why are we here?"

The boy downstairs whipped his head around again. This time he half stood.

"Father!" he said. "Do you hear it?"

He hears us! Alex thought, his heart in his throat.

But Michael and his father had already left their breakfast. Michael snatched up the lantern as his father reached for his gun. They both hurried out the door. The woman wiped her hands on her apron and followed.

Then Alex's ears picked up the sound. Hoofbeats drumming in the distance.

"Horses," Sophie whispered.

"It's the British!" Alex said. "We'd better get out of here!"

"Where?" Mattie asked. "They'll find us if we go back upstairs."

"That leaves downstairs," Alex stated. "Let's go!"

The kids crept the rest of the way down the steps. The kitchen door stood open.

Through the door, Alex could see the family gathered beside a dirt road.

Alex spotted thick bushes growing near the door. He gave Mattie a signal, and she nodded. The kids scrambled into the bushes before anyone could spot them. Mattie and Sophie huddled together while Alex crouched closest to the door.

Two horses galloped up the road to the house. Their hooves churned gravel as they headed toward the front door. For a second, Alex thought the animals were going to run right into the bushes where they were hidden.

But the riders pulled back on the reins and called "Whoa!"

Alex parted the leafy branches to peer out at the newcomers. A tall young man in a soldier's uniform jumped down from his horse. His cheeks were crisscrossed with scratches. Sweat dripped onto his collar.

"Captain Jack!" the man shouted. "What are you doing, running the legs off your horse? What happened to your face?"

"Tarleton and his men are right behind us," Captain Jack answered, his chest heaving. "They mean to capture members of our government! I rode all night to warn them. Had to stay off the road, so I went through the woods."

Now the second man dismounted. He wore a black coat, black knee pants, and white stockings. Loose strands from his reddish ponytail clung to his damp face.

Michael's father rushed to catch the reins of the man's horse. "Sir, can we offer you some breakfast?"

"Just water for our horses," said the red-haired man.

"Michael, run down to the creek," his father said.

"Yes, sir!" Michael dashed around to the back of the house.

"Will you let me tend those scratches?" the woman asked Captain Jack.

The young officer waved a hand. "We still have a long ride ahead of us."

"Tarleton's men rode into my yard as we left," the red-haired man said. "I hid the state papers just in time. We barely escaped."

"If they catch you," said Michael's father, "they'll arrest you."

"They have to catch us first," Captain Jack said.

Michael ran up with two sloshing pails of water. He set the buckets on the ground. The horses bent their necks and drank thirstily.

Sophie cried, "My horse!"

Before Mattie could stop her, Sophie burst through the bushes. She ran over to Captain Jack's horse and began stroking the animal's long mane.

"Oh, no!" Mattie cried.

"Sophie!" Alex shouted.

Everyone in the clearing stared at the figure petting the horse. In the shadowy lantern light, Sophie seemed bigger than she really was.

The red-haired man drew his sword.

Captain Jack whipped out his pistol.

"No!" Mattie and Alex yelled together.

"The enemy!" Captain Jack cried.

Alex leaped out of the bushes, dodging Captain Jack. He moved quickly, thanks to all those hours of soccer practice.

Mattie ran out and grabbed Sophie. The red-haired man looked startled.

"Alex!" Mattie pulled Sophie away. "The spyglass!"

He fished the spyglass from his pocket, extended it, and clutched Mattie's shirt.

Please let it work, he thought. He didn't like falling through the tunnel, but anything was better than facing a sharp sword! He gripped the spyglass tighter.

Alex saw Michael's eyes widen in amazement. Captain Jack and the red-haired man gawked at them, their mouths open.

Then Alex was swirling down the tunnel, tumbling through colors.

Bright lights like fireworks burst behind his eyelids. He couldn't see Mattie or Sophie. He hoped they were falling too.

Thump.

The soles of his tennis shoes hit something solid. Floorboards Alex opened his eyes, afraid they had landed back in the farmhouse.

The sky was sunny beyond the tower room windows. The sound of the lawn mower roared in the distance. Weak with relief, Alex saw his sisters next to him.

"We made it!" Mattie said.

Alex stared at the spyglass still in his

hand. Mattie snatched it away from him.

"We're not ever using this thing again!" she said. She walked over to the desk, jerked open the cubbyhole, and put the spyglass inside its wooden box.

"But that was cool," Alex protested.

"No, it wasn't," Mattie said. "It was dangerous."

"Not really," said Alex. "Only at the end. Matt, why do you think we went there?"

"I don't know. But we're never going again."

Sophie said to Ellsworth, "I told you we'd find the horse."

"What horse?" Mattie asked.

"You know the horse I keep seeing here?" Sophie answered. "The soldier was riding her."

5

Sophie's Horse

"Mattie! Alex!" Their mother's voice floated up from downstairs.

"Mom's coming!" Mattie exclaimed. "Get out before she finds us in here!"

Alex had already pushed open the bookcase door. "Go, Sophie!" he urged.

Sophie crawled through, dragging Ellsworth by one leg. Mattie hurried through behind her, then Alex.

They barely had time to arrange the books on the shelf before Mrs. Chapman appeared at the top of the stairs. She carried a stack of fluffy towels.

"Didn't you kids hear me?" she asked. "Where have you been?"

Alex glanced at Mattie. They couldn't answer that question even if they wanted to.

Sophie tugged at her mother's sleeve. "Mom! I saw the horse again! This time I petted her!"

"What horse, Pumpkin?" asked Mrs. Chapman.

Alex had to think fast. He pointed at the towels in his mother's arms. "Do these go in the yellow room? I'll take them."

"Oh thank you, dear," said his mother. She handed him the towels. "What are you three doing up here?"

Mattie cleared her throat. "We were looking for Mr. Jones."

"Mr. Jones checked out before breakfast. He's gone." Mrs. Chapman leaned against the doorjamb and peered into the room. "He made his own bed. It's like he was never here."

Now we'll never be able to ask him about the postcard, Alex thought. He raced past his mother and set the yellow towels on the bed. He was anxious to talk to Mattie and Sophie. But their mother had other ideas.

"We have two guests coming this afternoon," she was saying as he came out of the room. "The Dogwood Room is ready, but I need to clean the keeping room—"

"The what room?" Mattie asked.

"Oh, you know, the living room downstairs. In Colonial times, they called it a keeping room, because it was the place where people kept their necessities. I need to make sure it's clean for our guests, so I'm afraid I won't have time to help you two unpack your suitcases. Can you get started on your own? I'd like for your rooms to be tidy when the Kimbles arrive."

"Aw, Mom, do we have to?" asked Alex. "We're busy, uh, exploring."

"Just give it until lunchtime. You guys are great!" She kissed her fingertips, stamped Alex's, Sophie's, and Mattie's cheeks, then pattered back down the stairs.

"Come on," said Mattie. "We have work to do."

"But Mattie, we can't unpack right now," Alex said. "We need to talk about what just happened!"

"Shhh," Mattie said, as they stepped onto

the second floor landing. "Relax. We're not going to unpack—"

"I already unpacked Ellsworth's clothes," said Sophie. "And my crayons and paper."

Mattie wheeled around. "Bring me a sheet of paper, Soph. And a pencil! Quick!"

Sophie ran into her room.

"I don't get it," Alex said. "You're going to write a letter?"

"Better," Mattie said in a superior tone. "I'm going to figure out what just happened to us."

When Sophie returned with a slightly crumpled sheet of paper and a half-chewed pencil, Mattie ordered them all into her room. She closed the door.

On one side of the room, a white-washed dresser spanned the distance between two tall windows. Mattie's bunk bed stood against the opposite wall. Instead of a second bed, a desk sat beneath the top bunk, along with four red suitcases.

The kids sat cross-legged on the floor.

Mattie pulled over one of the suitcases, and set the paper on it. She printed *Mystery* at the top.

Sophie tilted her head, trying to read it. "What's that say?"

"Mystery," Mattie replied. "There must be a logical explanation for what happened."

"It was magic," Alex said. Then he added hesitantly, "Wasn't it?"

Mattie frowned at him. "Oh, Alex, grow up. You can't catch a rainbow. And there's no such thing as magic."

"Yes, there is," Sophie said.

"Magic happens in stories," Mattie told her briskly. "Not to regular people."

"What was it then, genius?" Alex said. "How did we get to that other place?"

"We dreamed it," Mattie said.

Alex snorted. "Three people dreaming the exact same dream?"

Even Mattie wasn't convinced. "All right, so it wasn't a dream. But it wasn't magic either."

Alex wanted to believe it was magic. Their lives would be so much more fun with magic. "If it's not magic, what was it?"

"I don't know. That's why I'm writing down what we do know," said Mattie. "One: the spyglass somehow caused us to go to a strange place."

"It wasn't just a strange place," Alex said. "It was another time. Remember how that boy and his father were dressed? They looked just like Mr. Jones. I think we went back to the time of the Revolutionary War."

Mattie looked at him for a moment and then said, "Okay. The spyglass caused us to go to a strange place and a strange time."

"Two," Alex said. "No time seemed to pass between when we left and when we got back."

"Right," Mattie said. "Can you think of anything else?"

"Only questions," said Alex. "Exactly where were we? And how did we get there?"

Mattie added *Where?* and *How?* in big letters and underlined the words.

"Magic," Sophie said again. "That's how."

Mattie shook her head. "It has to be something logical, like . . . um, a strong force from the electrical wires."

Alex got up. He walked around the suitcases over to the windows. Mattie and Sophie followed him.

"Not a power line in sight," Alex said. "I think Soph's right, Mattie. It must be magic."

Mattie scratched her chin. "No. It's got to be something logical. Maybe it has something to do with this place. Or this house." She headed for the door. "Let's go ask Mom. She's bound to know something."

They found their mother in the keeping room. She leaned over the coffee table as she fanned out a set of architecture magazines.

"Hi, kids," she said. "Did you finish unpacking?"

"Almost." Mattie casually picked up an apple from a wooden bowl on the table. She didn't meet her mother's eyes. "But we wanted to ask you a question first."

Mrs. Chapman straightened up, her hands on her hips. "All right."

Mattie polished the apple on her t-shirt and took a bite. "Have you ever noticed anything, uh, . . . strange about this house?"

Mrs. Chapman tilted her head. "Well, it makes strange noises now and then. But that's normal for an old house like this."

"How old exactly?" Alex asked.

"It's kind of hard to say," Mrs. Chapman replied. "Our house has been added on to over the years. I believe the tower was built around 1900. This part of the house dates back to Colonial times."

"So around the time of the Revolutionary War?" Mattie asked.

"Exactly!" Mrs. Chapman clapped her hands. "Oh Mattie, I'm thrilled you're taking an interest in the house at last. I knew you'd come to love it as much as Dad and I do."

She pointed at the row of bookcases

lining one wall. "You should check out those books I bought at the used bookstore. Most of them are about local history. I've been meaning to look through them to see if I can find out more about the house. I don't know much about what the original house looked like but," she tilted her head toward the hearth, "I know the fireplace here was part of the original Colonial keeping room."

The phone in the hall rang just then, and Mrs. Chapman left the keeping room to answer it.

Alex went over to the hearth. His ran his fingers over the alternating rows of rough-cut gray stones and smoky bricks. Then he glanced up at the mantel, painted a soft blue.

Alex clutched Mattie's arm.

"What?" she said.

"Our fireplace!" Alex said in an excited whisper. "The fireplace in the old-timey house was just like it!"

"So? Probably a lot of fireplaces look like ours."

"It wasn't like our fireplace," he said patiently. "It was our fireplace! Matt, don't you see? We visited our own house back in time."

No one spoke.

Finally Mattie said, "But how can we be sure?"

"Maybe the answer is in those old books, like Mom said." Alex walked over to the tall bookcases. "Where should we start?"

"How should I know?" Mattie finished the apple. She tossed the core in the wastebasket near the door. "The only thing I know about this place is that story Mr. Jones told us about the Virginian Paul Revere. Remember? The guy had a funny name."

"Jack something," Alex replied. Then his eyes widened. "Matt! The old-timey guy called the soldier Captain Jack! And Captain Jack said he rode all night to warn people the British were coming! It must be the same person Mr. Jones told us about."

"Look for books about Virginia history,"

Mattie said, dragging a footstool over to the first bookcase.

Alex groaned. "They're all about Virginia history."

"We have to start somewhere." She chose a heavy book and opened it on her knees.

Sophie sat on the floor between Mattie and Alex. "You pick," she said to Ellsworth. She guided the elephant's stuffed arm to a book bound in red leather. "That's a good one."

Sophie cracked the cover open. The book smelled like the tower room. Like old secrets.

She pretended to read. "Once upon a time a soldier got on his horse. The horse was a gray. She was a girl horse. They rode through the woods."

Mattie stared at the book spread across her sister's lap. "Alex, look at this."

They gathered around Sophie. An old-fashioned drawing showed a soldier in a Revolutionary War uniform on a horse. Under the drawing was written, *The Midnight Ride of Captain Jack Jouett.*

"That must be him!" Alex said. "Sophie, how did you find this?"

"Ellsworth found it," Sophie said. "Look, there's my horse."

Mattie read the fine print under the caption, "Captain Jack Jouett on Sallie, his famous gray mare."

Alex gasped. "Soph's been seeing Captain Jouett's horse in our yard all along!"

Mattie stared at Sophie. "But how?"

"Magic! We told you." Alex grabbed the book and skimmed the entire entry. "Listen. It's just like what we saw. This Jack Jouett guy heard some British soldiers talking in a tavern. They were going to kidnap Virginia's governor, Thomas Jefferson, and other men who signed the Declam—I mean, Declaration of Independence."

Alex angled the book so Mattie could read too. "On June 3rd, 1781," she murmured, "Jack Jouett rode forty miles through the woods to warn members of the General Assembly. Colonel Tarleton and his men were in Governor Jefferson's yard when Jouett and Governor Jefferson escaped with their lives."

Alex looked up. "The old-timey people kept calling that red-haired man 'governor.' "

Mattie's eyes grew wide. "You don't think that man who tried to stab us was—"

"Thomas Jefferson?" Alex jumped up and down. "Yeah! We met Thomas Jefferson!" He chopped the air with a soccer kick. "We showed him!"

"Stop it," Mattie said. "This is serious. If we really did go back in time . . . and I'm not saying we did . . . but if we did, what if we messed it up somehow? Thomas Jefferson thought we were spies. What happened after we left?" She leaned closer to Alex. "What if we messed up history?"

Alex let out a breath. "We have to go back. It's the only way to find out."

"No! We'd probably go right back to where we left off. Jack Jouett and Thomas Jefferson were after us, remember?"

"Who made you queen?" Alex was tired of her bossiness. He stood up.

"Maybe we can find out if anything else happened in another book," Mattie said.

"Forget the books," he said. "C'mon, Soph. Let's go back in time!" He sprinted out of the room.

"Okay!" Sophie snatched up Ellsworth and dashed after him.

"Wait!" Mattie shoved the books to the floor and ran after them.

Alex raced up the curving staircase, pounded down the guest room hallway, and up the steps to the third floor.

He and Sophie were crawling through the secret panel when Mattie came racing up the stairs.

"Wait!" she called, crawling through the panel on her hands and knees. "You don't know what will happen—"

Alex fetched the box from the desk and took out the spyglass. "You're scared, aren't you? You act all smart about magic not being real. But you do believe, same as Sophie and me! Only you're a scaredy-cat!"

He held the spyglass in his right hand.

Sophie gripped his shirt.

"Alex—!" Mattie clutched his hand.

Alex's fingers tingled, and grew warm. In an instant, he whirled down the glittery chute.

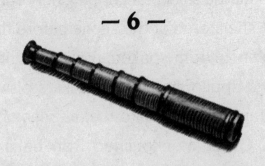

6

The Second Trip

Once more it was night, but far from dark. Lights like Fourth of July fireworks burst in the black sky. B*oom*! K*aboom*!

But the kids were not at a Fourth of July picnic. And they weren't in their house either. They were on an open field somewhere. A cold, drizzling rain dampened their clothes.

"I told you the spyglass wouldn't work

right!" Mattie said. Still gripping her brother's hand, she stared at the scene before them.

Men in rain-soaked uniforms dipped sponge-tipped staffs into buckets of water, then rammed them into the muzzles of cannons. Other men pushed iron balls into cannons and fired.

Alex yanked his hand free before Mattie could crush it. "This is way better than going back in time to our house!"

"But where are we?"

"In the middle of a battle!" he replied.

Every flash lit up a field lined with different kinds of cannons.

The air was thick with black smoke. Gunpowder smelled like a million lit matches.

Cannonballs screamed toward a nearby town. Alex could see houses with broken windows and holes in rooftops. From a crude fort in front of the town, cannonballs flew back in their direction.

Blue-coated officers on horses raced around Alex and his sisters, slashing curved swords. Their faces were tense and tired. One man in a plumed hat and red-lined cape nearly ran Alex over on his horse.

Mattie pushed Sophie behind her. "Alex, we've got to get out of here!" she yelled over the noise.

"It's okay," he said. "We're in the Revolutionary War! All these guys are patriots—our side!"

"And the British are firing at them!" Mattie pushed her wet bangs off her forehead. "We have to go back home, Alex. Give me the spyglass!"

"No." Alex shoved the spyglass in his pocket. For once, he was not letting her win.

"We're not going back. Not yet. We must be here for a reason."

A cannonball screamed across the sky and landed with a boom that rocked the field.

"What reason?" Mattie asked. "To get squashed by a cannonball? Come on!"

Mattie pulled Alex and Sophie across the field, away from the cannons, toward a grove of trees. Canvas tents dotted the landscape.

Alex stepped on something soft. A soggy hat lay in the mud.

He picked it up, shook off the rainwater, and put it on. The hat was too big, but he didn't care. He wanted to look like a patriot.

He was hunting for one of those curved swords in the same area when a voice said in his ear, "Have you something for me?"

Straightening, Alex looked into the eyes

of a boy Mattie's age, maybe a little older. He wore his brown hair tied back in a low pony-tail. His face was grimy with gun powder.

"Something for you?" Alex asked. "Like what?"

The boy stared at Alex's jeans and t-shirt. Then he looked at Mattie and Sophie. "Do you hail from the town?"

"What town?" Mattie replied.

"You must be from the country," the boy said. "People dress mighty peculiar in these parts."

"Where we come from we do dress kind of funny—" Alex said. His voice broke off as another cannon blasted nearby.

"You'd best go home, then," the boy said.

"Um . . ." Alex began, "we're not exactly sure where we are."

The boy's eyes grew round. "Don't know where you are? Are you daft? Did you get hit on the head?"

"We sort of . . . dropped in," Mattie said. "And now we're lost."

"Why, you're near Yorktown!" the boy said. "We've been firing on the Redcoats for ten solid days."

Alex remembered Mr. Jones had been on his way to Yorktown. He and other re-enactors were soldiers in a play version of the battle.

"What is the date?" Alex asked the boy.

"The seventeenth day of October."

"And the year?"

"1781," the boy replied. "Are you sure you weren't conked on the head? I could take you to the general's doctor."

"We're okay," Alex said.

The boy shot him a puzzled look.

"I mean, all right," Alex corrected himself. People in 1781 didn't say "okay."

Just then a soldier galloped up on a black horse. He sawed the reins so sharply his horse reared and pawed the air. The soldier remained in the saddle.

"Oh! Can I pet the horse?" Sophie asked.

Mattie kept a firm grip on her sister's overall strap. "Absolutely not!"

"Will Thomas!" the soldier shouted at the

boy. The man withdrew a square of paper from his silver-buttoned jacket and handed it to Will. "Take this to the general. Make haste!" The soldier tore off into the smoke.

"Are you a spy?" Alex asked.

"Indeed not!" Will said, indignant. "I am a messenger for the Continental Army. And I must deliver this."

"Can I go with you?" asked Alex. Will Thomas had the coolest job, and he was just a kid!

Now Will gave them a suspicious once-over. "How do I know you aren't spies? You certainly don't look like Americans."

Alex lifted his chin. "We are Americans. I'm Alex and these are my sisters, Mattie and Sophie."

"Besides, we're children," Mattie said. "How could we be spies?"

Will seemed to consider this. Then he said, "All right. Come with me. But we must hurry."

He set off at a furious pace in the rain, leading them toward a group of tents in the distance. They squelched through a marsh and waded across a creek.

"Are we winning?" Alex asked, half-running to keep up. "The battle, I mean."

Will laughed. "I'll say! Old Cornwallis thought he was so smart, building puny forts around Yorktown. But the general was smarter. When we got here, we dug trenches near the British forts. We hid in the trenches and fired on the enemy from close range."

"Who is Cornwallis?" Alex asked. He'd heard the name before.

"Lord Cornwallis?" Will replied. "Why, he's the British commander in the South. He's been pestering patriots in the Southern states for months. But he is no match for the Americans and the French."

"There are French soldiers here too?" asked Mattie.

"French warships are moored in the York River on the other side of Yorktown," said Will. "Many French troops fight with us. They too hate the British."

Mattie held Sophie's hand so her sister wouldn't fall behind.

"How long have you been in the war?" Mattie asked Will. A shell streaked across the sky.

"I joined the general this summer in New Jersey. I would have joined in '75, but I was too young. My father was in the army too. He took sick the winter of '77 at Valley Forge."

"What happened to him?" Alex asked, almost afraid to hear the answer.

"He had to go home," Will replied. "His feet froze, and now he can barely walk. But I'm here."

"Aren't you afraid?" asked Mattie.

Will shook his head. "I've carried messages in many battles. I have never been afraid. I am more afraid of losing this war."

Alex wished they could tell Will Thomas that Americans would win the Revolutionary War. But Will already thought they were weird. Besides, if he did, he might mess up the way things were supposed to go at Yorktown.

"Faster," Will urged them. "The general needs this message right away."

Before Alex could ask "General who?" Will's right leg skidded into a hole up to his knee, and he went down with a yell.

Alex helped him up. "Are you okay?"

Will put his weight on his foot and winced.

He didn't seem to notice Alex's use of the strange word. "I may have twisted my ankle."

"You can't walk?" Mattie asked.

He took a tentative step, then sank to the ground with a groan. "Ooh, it hurts. What am I going to do? If I could find another messenger, I would let him carry it to the general."

"You don't have time," Alex said. "Why don't you let me do it?"

"No! It's too dangerous!" Mattie said to her brother.

Will rubbed his ankle. "I don't have much choice. But you cannot go to the general's tent dressed in those strange clothes. The guards will never let you through."

"I'll wear your jacket. I've already got one of those hats." Alex did a little dance. He was going to be part of the Battle of Yorktown!

"It might work," Will said slowly. He jiggled his foot and gasped.

"Let me wrap your ankle," Mattie offered. "Alex, give me your shirt. I did this once in soc—" She stopped.

Alex knew she started to say "soccer." He made a big show of pulling his shirt over his head. Mattie ripped a strip from the bottom. She wound it around Will's swollen ankle and tied the ends.

Then Will slipped out of his jacket and boots. He put on Alex's torn t-shirt and tennis shoes. He touched the rubber soles gingerly. "Interesting."

Alex shrugged into the mud-spattered jacket and slipped his feet into Will's boots.

Will's long jacket made Alex's modern jeans less obvious.

"Where do I go?" he asked, tucking the note in his jacket.

Will pointed. "Straight. You'll cross another creek. Then you'll see the French guns. The French general's tent is first. Our headquarters are just beyond. The general's tent is the biggest."

Alex set off without hesitation. Then he glanced behind him. He felt strange leaving Mattie and Sophie behind. Would they be okay?

Mattie and Sophie were sitting on a log, looking at him. The rain was letting up, but the wind grew stronger. Smoke streamed across the battlefield, stinging Alex's eyes.

"You must go with your brother," Alex heard Will say.

"But we can't leave you!" Mattie protested. "You're hurt."

"I'll be fine," Will said. He waved a hand. "Go! And hurry! Battles can be won or lost with a message."

Mattie and Sophie ran to catch up with Alex.

"Alex! Wait! We're coming too!" Mattie said.

Alex was relieved. As much as he wanted glory, he didn't feel that brave.

The three kids ran toward the creek.

Will's boots were too big. Alex had a hard time walking in them. He felt himself sinking in mud up over his bootlaces. He tried to yank his right foot out, but it sank deeper.

"Alex!" Mattie shrieked behind him. "What is this stuff? It's like quicksand!"

"We're in a swamp, that's all," he said, with more confidence than he felt. "Lift your feet slowly, don't move fast."

At last, they came to the churning creek. The swamp wasn't as bad on the other side of the creek. They tramped down reeds and cattails to make a path. With a burst of energy, Alex began running up the rise toward the tents.

He passed several cannons and heard men speaking a foreign language. French, he guessed. He dashed past a large tent surrounded by more men speaking French.

Everyone seemed excited about something. No one paid any attention to three kids wearing strange clothes.

Then he saw another group of tents, just as Will said. Men in blue uniforms patrolled the area around the largest tent. They carried guns on their shoulders.

Alex swallowed. Would he make it past the guards? Even if he did, what would they do when they saw Mattie and Sophie?

At that moment, another messenger dashed up on horseback. The guards rushed over. The messenger dismounted in one swift motion and tossed his reins to a guard.

Alex, Mattie, and Sophie saw their chance. Together, they scurried up to the tent and pushed aside the flap.

When they looked inside the tent, they gasped.

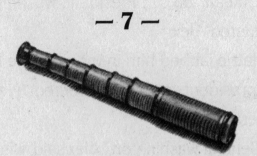

7

The General

A tall man in a blue coat, white pants, and knee boots stood by a desk.

Alex had seen the man's face on quarters, dollar bills, and in history books. It was probably the most famous face in American history.

"George Washington!" Alex breathed.

The man gave Alex a sharp, disapproving frown. "I beg your pardon?"

"I mean, uh . . . President Washington!" stammered Alex.

Mattie jabbed him in the ribs. "He hasn't been president yet!" she whispered. "He's still a general."

"General Washington," Alex said, whipping the folded paper from his borrowed jacket. "I have a message for you, sir." He saluted, but with the wrong hand.

General Washington took the paper, giving Alex a suspicious glance. "I don't recognize you as one of my messengers. And who are these females?"

"Females?" Mattie said.

Alex knew his bossy sister did not like being called a female. "These are my sisters, General, sir," Alex said. "Will Thomas hurt his ankle on the field, sir. So he asked me to bring the message to you."

"Will Thomas I know well," said General Washington. "If he entrusted you to bring this message, than so will I."

Alex noticed George Washington's white hair was pulled back into a ponytail. He thought he looked too young to have white hair. Then he remembered that men wore powdered wigs back in Colonial times.

He glanced around the tent. A map was spread on the desk. Holding the map down at one corner was a brass telescope. He wondered if Washington's spyglass was magic too. Probably not, or George Washington would have sent the British army to another time period.

Meanwhile, the general had unfolded the paper and was examining it by the light of a pierced tin lantern. Most of the page was printed, as if it had been cut from a book.

Columns of handwritten numbers and words marched down the margins.

"That's code, isn't it?" said Alex. "How come you didn't use invisible ink?"

Washington gave him a piercing glance. "What do you know about my sympathetic stain?"

"Your what?" Then Alex remembered who he was addressing. "Er—nothing, sir."

"It is customary," the general said severely, "to wait outside." Then he reached for a sheaf of well-thumbed papers. He referred to the papers as he read the message.

"That must be a code book!" Mattie whispered.

"Good news, indeed," murmured Washington. Alex couldn't tell if he was speaking to them or himself. "General Cornwallis tried to escape last night by boat.

But the fierce rainstorm forced him back to Yorktown."

He put down the papers and looked up. "You're still here?" he asked. But this time his voice wasn't quite as stern. "Follow me."

The kids and the general stepped outside the tent. The rain had stopped. The air seemed freshly washed. The sky glowed a faint pink in the east. Overhead, meteors streaked in graceful arcs.

"Look!" Sophie exclaimed. "Shooting stars!"

George Washington nodded and smiled.

He turned to Alex. "Thank you for delivering the message." Then he went back into his tent.

"What now?" asked Mattie.

"Let's go see if Will is okay," Alex said.

They walked back toward the battlefield.

The cannons were louder than ever. The ground shook beneath their feet with each boom.

Sophie covered her ears. "Mattie, I don't like all this noise."

"Neither do I," Mattie said. "Let's go home now."

"We can't," Sophie said. "We're supposed to stay."

"Stay for what?" asked Alex, yelling to be heard over the roar of guns.

But Sophie did not reply. She stepped over holes and puddles with her short legs, hugging Ellsworth protectively. They crossed the swamp carefully and hurried back to where they had left Will Thomas.

He was sitting on an empty ammunition box. "What happened? Did you deliver the message?" He stood up slowly.

"Careful!" Mattie rushed to his side.

Will smiled. "I think my ankle is better. See?" He took a few slow but steady steps.

While Alex and Will exchanged clothes again, Alex told him what they had learned at General Washington's headquarters.

"Old Cornwallis is a goner, all right!" Will said, buttoning his jacket. "Alexander, thank you for getting that message through. It was very important."

"The message was in code, wasn't it?" said Alex. "We saw General Washington using a code book. He said something about—what was it? Sympathetic strain?"

"Stain," Will corrected. "Sympathetic stain. It is an invisible ink. General Washington orders his spies to use it. You have to use a special chemical to make the message appear. He's very cautious about letting messages fall into wrong hands."

"He didn't use any chemical," Mattie said. "He just looked up words in his code book."

"Things must be happening too fast," said Will.

Will led them around the edge of the battlefield. Americans fired muskets from trenches. The British fired a few return shots over the wall of the fort.

Alex clenched his fists. Why didn't the British give up and go back to England? They were wrong trying to keep America from being free.

"Look!" Will pointed.

The kids squinted to see through the smoke. A small figure in red climbed onto a ledge on top of the wall. He carried a drum. While the guns blasted all around him, the boy began to beat the drum.

"He's going to be hurt!" Mattie cried. "Somebody do something!"

Just then a British soldier joined the drummer boy. He waved a white flag. The drummer boy kept drumming. The firing slowed as American soldiers saw them.

"Cornwallis has surrendered!" Will cried joyfully.

Gradually, the guns grew quiet. The American soldiers sent up a rowdy cheer.

"Yay!" Alex cheered with them and tossed his hat in the air.

Suddenly an officer on horseback charged along the lines of men.

It was General Washington!

"Resume your positions!" he shouted to his troops. "Posterity will do the huzzahs for us!"

"What did he say?" Mattie asked Will.

"He said that history will cheer for what we did this day," Will answered.

Yes, it will, Alex thought. Once again, he was tempted to tell Will that future Americans were very grateful. But of course, he couldn't.

"General Washington is going back to his headquarters," said Will. "Something is happening."

The kids made their way across the battlefield toward Washington's camp. Although the Americans had quit shooting, the soldiers remained on the field.

No one noticed four children skirting the trenches. All eyes were fixed on the British drummer boy and the British officer who waved the white cloth. Americans had blind-folded them and led them through the lines of soldiers. The boy did not stop drumming.

The kids hid behind a wagon. They

watched the little parade stopped in front of headquarters. A messenger hurried into General Washington's tent with a folded paper.

"I'll wager that is the news we've been longing for!" Will said with glee. "The official surrender from Cornwallis! I'm going to go write my father!" He dashed toward a row of tents.

"We should go home," Mattie whispered to Alex. "Mom and Dad will be worried sick about us. We've been gone for hours."

"But we were only gone for a few minutes last time," Alex said. "I want to stay and see what happens next!"

Sophie tugged on Alex's sleeve. "It's time to go."

He sighed and pulled the spyglass from his jeans pocket.

Mattie gazed at the rapt crowd. "Let's

go now, while nobody is paying attention to us."

Alex held out the spyglass. Mattie grasped one end. Sophie clung to the other end.

Alex squeezed his eyes shut. This time he didn't mind the flashing lights and falling motion. He trusted the spyglass to take him safely home.

8

The Letter in the Desk

Alex opened his eyes. His feet were firmly on the floor again. He heard his father's weed trimmer. More faintly, his mother's voice from the front hall, still talking on the phone.

Yes! It was still morning! They had not been missed.

"That was fun!" Alex said to Mattie. He twirled the spyglass.

Mattie looked at him as if he'd lost his

mind. "It was not fun, Alex. We were in a war! Both times we used the spyglass, we were sent back in time to danger. I think we ought to put it back in the desk and leave it there."

"Are you crazy?" said Alex. "We're supposed to use the spyglass. Aren't we, Sophie?"

Sophie hugged Ellsworth to her chest. "Yes."

"Are we supposed to get killed, too?" Mattie shot back.

"Mattie, we were sent back there for a reason," Alex said. "We helped Will when he couldn't walk. What if General Washington hadn't got that message about Cornwallis trying to escape? We gave it to him!

"Plus what we did was educational!" Alex went on. "Better than any video or field trip." He grinned. "Think of the great reports we'll be able to write!"

"Are you kidding?" Mattie set her lips in a firm line. "If we tell anyone what happened to us, they'll think we're crazy. We can't ever use this thing again." She walked over to the desk, opened the cubbyhole, and put the spyglass in its box.

Alex tried to open the cubbyhole again, but Mattie blocked him.

"You can't do that!" he yelled.

"I can and I did. I'm the oldest." She flashed him her don't-mess-with-me expression.

Alex stomped his foot. "You can't keep Sophie and me out of the tower room. We'll use the spyglass any time we want!"

"It won't work without the three of us," Mattie said.

"You're wrong!" Alex whirled, opened the cubbyhole, and took out the spyglass again. "Soph, grab the other end."

Sophie touched the eyepiece.

He waited for the spyglass to grow warm, for his fingers to tingle. But the brass case remained cool, and his hand felt normal.

"Told you," Mattie said smugly.

"I'm taking the spyglass down to my room," he said.

But when he approached the bookcase-door, he dropped the brass tube. He picked it up, but dropped it again.

"If you keep dropping it, you'll break it," said Mattie. "What's the matter with you?"

"It's not me. The spyglass is—it's jumping out of my hand," Alex said.

"It doesn't want to go to your room," Sophie said. "It has to stay in the tower."

"See? We're not supposed to use it again." Mattie took the spyglass away from him and put it back in the desk. "Let's get out of here."

Alex stomped downstairs. Nothing made him madder than when Miss Know-It-All was right.

They met their mother going into the kitchen.

"There you are, Mattie," said Mrs. Chapman. "That was the Kimbles on the phone. They'll be here in less than an hour. Since you're nearly done unpacking, would you mind helping me dust the dining room, please? I want to make sure the house is spotless for our guests." She turned to Alex. "Maybe Sophie can help you finish unpacking your suitcases?"

"Sure, Mom," Alex said. "C'mon, Soph."

Sophie skipped up the stairs ahead of him. "See you later, Mattie."

Alex didn't say anything. He was glad Mattie got stuck dusting. That's what she deserved.

Alex trudged up the stairs and stepped into his new room. The space was much bigger than his room in Maryland. His battered maple desk sat under the only window in the room. His twin bed with its familiar blue and gold plaid comforter, nestled in the corner. Dad had left Alex's giant orange duffle bag on the bed. It felt good to have all his things in one place again.

Sophie walked Ellsworth's stuffed legs along the top of the desk. She looked at Alex. "Ellsworth had fun on our trip."

"Yeah, me too." Alex unzipped the duffle bag, pulled out his Goalie of the Year trophy, and set it on the desk. Soccer didn't seem as exciting as it used to, now that they'd found the spyglass. He'd have to convince Mattie to try it again. But how?

Suddenly the door flew open.

Mattie stood in the doorway and yelled, "Alex! Sophie! Come, quick!"

Sophie flew out the door, but Alex moved more slowly.

"What is it now?" he asked sarcastically as he sauntered across the floor. "Does the queen wish us to—"

"The tower room," was all Mattie said. She sped through the hallway and up to the third floor.

Alex and Sophie pounded up the stairs behind her.

Mattie dropped to her knees and pivoted the secret panel, rattling the books on the shelves. She scurried inside and waved the others through.

"I thought we weren't allowed up here anymore," Alex said.

"Be quiet and look." She held out the postcard with the painting of the battle scene.

"So," he said. "That's the postcard Mr. Jones sent."

"I found it under the sideboard while I was dusting. It must have fallen out of the outgoing mail basket somehow. Look at it again. Does the picture seem familiar now?"

Alex stared. "It's the battle of Yorktown," he finally said. "I recognize the British fort in the background! The one that drummer boy stood on. How—?"

"Wait, there's more." Mattie turned the postcard over. "Read the signature again."

"Will." Alex looked up at Mattie. "That must be Will Thomas! He wrote to his father!"

"It has to be," Mattie said. "But I don't understand how."

Sophie stood on tiptoes to see the card.

"First Mr. Jones wrote it, then Will did," she said. "It changed."

"Do you know how?" Mattie asked.

Sophie shook her head. "But we were supposed to read it."

"You mean the card was never meant to be mailed?" Mattie asked. "We were supposed to find it?"

Sophie nodded.

Mattie looked at Alex. "Some of this is starting to make sense. Mr. Jones's postcard was a hint where we would go when we used the spyglass."

"So Mr. Jones started the whole thing," said Alex. "And if we had paid attention to the postcard—after it changed, we would have known we were going to that battle."

Leaning against the desk, Mattie frowned. "But there's one thing I still don't understand.

Why did we take that trip back to our old house? That wasn't part of the Battle of Yorktown."

"Maybe we were supposed to see Captain Jack and Thomas Jefferson at our house back in the seventeen hundreds," Alex said. "So we'd know the spyglass could take us back in time. To prove we weren't dreaming."

"Maybe," Mattie said thoughtfully, "we saw something important in our old house, and we don't know what it is yet."

"Do you think we'll get to go on another trip?" Alex asked. "I want to go back in time and spy again!"

"Me too," said Mattie. She sounded surprised at herself.

"Why don't we try it now?" Alex's face lit up. "Let's see where the spyglass will take us next! Come on, Matt!"

"It won't work," Sophie said. "We have to wait for a postcard."

"Do you really think we'll get another one?" Alex asked.

Sophie didn't answer. She walked over to the old desk and pulled the knob of the bottom drawer.

"Soph, what are you doing?" Mattie asked. "You know that drawer is stuck."

"No, it's not," Sophie said.

The drawer slid open easily. She reached in and pulled out several sheets of paper with writing on them.

"Here," Sophie said, giving the papers to Mattie. "You read better than me."

"What's it say?" Alex said.

Mattie finished reading before answering. Then she announced dramatically, "I knew it."

Alex's brows lifted. "Knew what?"

"I knew it all along," she said breezily. "The spyglass, the postcard, Mr. Jones. All of it. Magic. Definitely magic."

"I told you," said Sophie.

"Of course it's magic!" Alex said, losing his patience. "Are you going to tell us what's on those papers?" Sometimes he thought he had the most irritating sister in the world!

Mattie was clearly in no hurry. "And you know what else?"

"What?" said Alex and Sophie together.

She grinned. "We will never, ever be bored in this house again!"

Then, and only then, did she read them what was on the paper.

Dear Mattie, Alex, and Sophie,

I hope you enjoyed your first trip using the spyglass. Even Alex found that history could be pretty exciting!

You already knew some facts about Colonial America, and you learned more on your trip. But I wouldn't be a very good Travel Guide if I didn't answer some questions you might have.

Our country was once a colony of Great Britain. Even though King George lived in England, he ruled America. He made laws that were unpopular.

In 1773, British lawmakers passed a tax on tea. One night, some colonists dressed as Mohawk Indians and crept aboard British ships in Boston Harbor. They dumped boxes of tea into the water to protest the tax.

Of course, King George was angry. He sent troops to America. Americans decided to fight for freedom.

Men from twelve colonies met in Philadelphia, Pennsylvania. They chose George Washington to command the new Continental Army. Next, the colonies declared their freedom from Britain. Thomas Jefferson wrote the Declaration of Independence. On July 4, 1776, Congress officially accepted the document.

The Revolutionary War raged from New England to the Southern states for more than six years. On June 3, 1781, Captain Jack Jouett overheard British soldiers planning to kidnap Governor Thomas Jefferson and other patriots. Jouett raced his horse through the woods to warn the governor and other members of the Virginia Assembly. The British soldiers were angry when their plan was foiled.

Four months later, General Washington faced General Charles Cornwallis, the British general who had been fighting in the South. Washington trapped Cornwallis and his troops at Yorktown, a small Virginia town on the York River. With the help of the French, the Americans fired on the British. French ships in the river also attacked Cornwallis's troops. At last, the British surrendered.

The war was not over. It took two more years before Great Britain signed a peace treaty with the United States of America. General Washington was chosen to be president of the nation, and our country was free at last!

Now, I suppose you're wondering why you three were chosen to witness some of these events. I can't answer everything, but you will find out in due time. All I can say right now is: yes, Mattie, it is magic.

Since you've been to the Revolutionary War, would you like to go some place else? You don't really get to choose, but I'll give you a tiny hint, just this once: your next trip has to do with another old house. In the meantime, I'm leaving you instructions to help you brush up on your spying skills.

Now I must close. Don't look for me next time. Your Travel Guide will be someone new, and he—or she—will arrive when you least expect it.

Yours in time,
"Mr. Jones"

TIME SPIES MISSION NO. 1
WRITE LIKE A SPY

Spies on both sides of the Revolutionary War sent secret messages. George Washington's chief spy, Benjamin Tallmadge, made up a number code. Only Washington, Tallmadge, and two spies had copies of the code book.

A doctor, James Jay, invented a new kind of invisible ink for George Washington. Washington ordered his spies to write in code, using the invisible ink. They wrote on pages torn from books or advertisements. A message written in code with invisible ink was practically impossible for the British to read!

Until your next adventure, your mission is to learn how to write like a spy. Good luck!

YOU WILL NEED:

Bottled lemon juice
Artist's paintbrush
Paper
Lightbulb in lamp
Top-Secret Code Book

WHAT YOU DO:

1. Dip your brush into the lemon juice.

2. Write this message in invisible ink:
   1234 7859 5678 4321 2468 9753?

3. Let the paper dry.

4. Pass it to a friend along with your code book.

5. Tell your friend to hold the paper over the lightbulb. The lemon juice will turn brown, and the words will appear.

TOP-SECRET CODE BOOK

Use these codes, or make up your own!

Everyday words

1212	can
1234	school
2468	today
2613	go
5678	is
4321	awful
6515	you
7080	and
7859	lunch
8341	I
9753	trade

Revolutionary words

38	attack
192	fort
223	gold
613	soldier
635	troops
659	victory
679	wind
686	wharf
700	water
711	Washington
739	Virginia